I0726545

Thanks to my Parents, Family, John, Beth and Esme.Stu,Catherine and my friends, proofreader Aimee Youles, Illustrator Samuel Batley, and of course the fantastic team at Great Writers Media.

Dedication to my Father Terence Gregson, the greatest storyteller
of all time who I learned everything from.

THE TALES OF LANEHOUSE

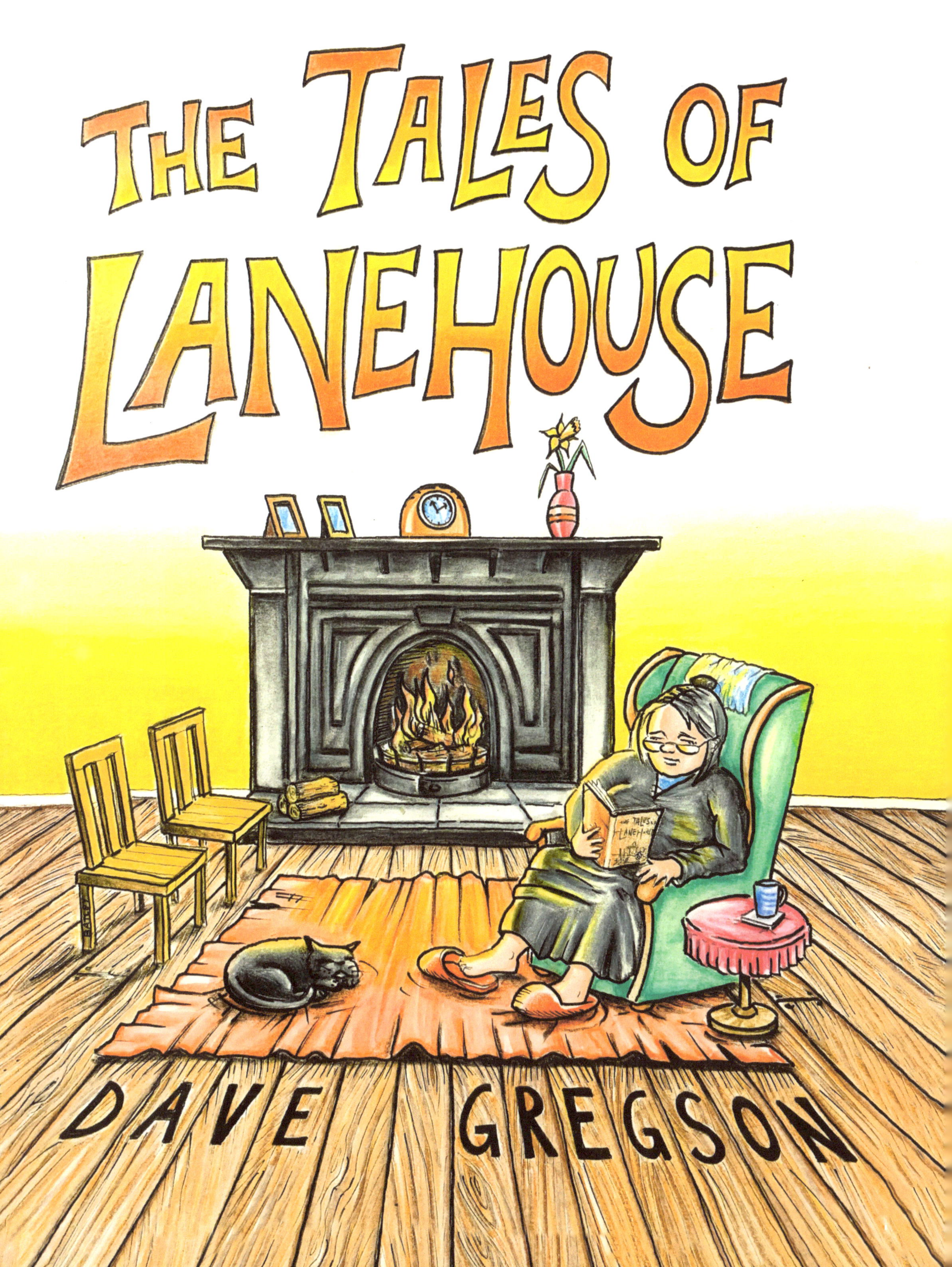

THE TALES OF
LANEHOUSE
DAVE GREGSON

Copyright © 2021 by Dave Gregson

All rights reserved. This book or any portion thereof may not be reproduced or used in any manner whatsoever without the express written permission of the publisher except for the use of brief quotation in a book review.

Inquiries and Book Orders should be addressed to:

Great Writers Media
Email: info@greatwritersmedia.com
Phone: (302) 918-5570
24A Trolley Square #1580 Wilmington, DE 19806-3334, USA

ISBN: 978-1-961416-59-8 (sc)
ISBN: 978-1-961416-60-4 (eb)

Rev 05/05/2021

Tales of Lanehouse...
The Journey Begins

He woke up on this day, and on this very day, only he knew that he had to return to the house in the terraced row at the top the village, and journey back to Trawden. He left early and the day was slightly grey with that very fine rain almost with the texture of mist that seems to endlessly blow into you out of a bleak and ashen grey sky.

He decided to go by public transport, he could have driven but this gave it more of an authentic feel and more time to think, the journey by bus had four stages, he remembered this from the old days when his Great Uncle John used to visit in his flat cap and old rain coat, the familiar fragrant aroma of mellow virginia pipe tobacco.

He passed the border into Lancashire, where the atmosphere seemed to change to become both a sense of foreboding and inner apprehensive excitement. The bleak and desolate Pennines passing by the bus window but they seemed more reassuring than bleak, barren and desolate. How amazing seeing that old town hall in Colne looked still the same as he remembered and the little cosy cafe on the corner was still there, memories of pint mugs of tea for the adults, sarsaparilla for him and his sister and the hot bowls of pie and peas. There was no time to stop though, it was now time for the final leg of the journey, the bus from Colne to Trawden. The air seemed suddenly clearer, fresher and almost inviting, as if offering reassurance that despite the few difficult years he had experienced, that was over now and he was OK. The old telephone box was still there too on the way to Trawden, a chortle to himself as he thought that there was no internet, mobiles or even television in the days when he sat in his Grandmas house.

He saw it clearly, the tiny terraced house that had been home to the family for many generations until 1979, where the tin baths were used by the fireplace and the real fire kept the whole family warm on those cold winter nights. The old rug by the fireside, the ancient cast iron stove and fireplace.

The old red hessayon rug by the fire and Grandma sitting there in her black dress in the old chair by the fireside recanting tales to a captivated audience, fantastic stories and tales of mystery and imagination. The terraced house on the street "Lanehouse".

Tales From Lanehouse .... Arrival

The Narrator had arrived back in Trawden or to be given its full name Trawden Forest Village, harking back to an ancient time when the village of Trawden, surrounding areas and the land across the Pennines and forest of Bowland would have been just. A vast expanse of ancient woodlands with huge gnarled trees and teeming with wildlife from years ago such as deer, wild boar, brown bears and of course Canis lupus or the grey wolf. There is always magic and enchantment around forests and the mysteries of the unknown. This magic was always present and around in the Trawden the Narrator knew so well.

Recanted in tales from within Lanehouse, his Grandmother's house,in front of that huge black iron fireplace, coal fires roaring, sat on the old hessayon rug with an ample supply of cakes, cups of tea and glasses or sarsaparilla for him and his brother.

The bed and breakfast he stayed at was quiet nondescript but friendly and cosy and a small family business, the owners did not know of his connection to Trawden but they didn't need to either, his mission was covert in that sense.

Walking up Church Street the Narrator was awestruck at how little had changed, the old stone edifice of his Great Uncles and Great Aunts house was still there, St Marys Church right at the top of the hill. The Narrator walked past the cottages of Boulsworth Drive where his Aunt Edith would always make them welcome with a friendly smile and an energy that knew no bounds.

The Narrator saw Lanehouse come into view, it was a bright sunny day, the rain had long passed and the blue sky's radiated a beautiful sunny day,which in his mind's eye he thought was shining especially brilliantly down on him and Trawden Village. Those long hot summer days s of yesteryear when generations of children played out in the street, down by the stream throwing coins into the fountain, feeding the ducks and chickens down at the pen or local school or climbing on the ancient dry stone walls that had covered the County of Lancashire for the past two hundred years. Lanehouse itself was strikingly like a friendly stone face smiling at him and warmly welcoming his return.

9

The Window Watchers
Curious Warning

To glimpse the village green through the parlour window Mrs. Hilton had to manhandle the heavy leather armchair forward then perch painfully on the edge of the seat. Only a small section of the green was visible – the path that led from the high street to the general store. Alice Hilton was not at ease. Her face was drawn, fingers digging nervously into the chair arms.

He was late! Mr. Keating was late! She didn't know his christian name. In fact, she knew nothing about him. Expect that he had arrived in the village a week – exactly one week – earlier; that he had rented the isolated cottage down Lamb Lane; that he was obviously retired; that he walked with a vigorous, purposeful, upright movement; that each day he crossed that stretch of green at exactly 10 o'clock and that this morning he hadn't. And, also, that there was some sort of undefined affinity – that she felt.

Tensely, Mrs. Hilton glanced at the clock on the mantle place. The hard knot of anxiety in her chest tightened. Partly, it was simply irritation that she couldn't explain this affinity – this pervasive feeling to herself. She had always been a practical person – a matter of personal pride. An identity. Not overly emotional – and certainly not prey to sudden passions. That was not a word she would use about herself – nor, she was quite sure, would anybody who knew her.

A quick edgy, almost alarmed, glance through the window. Nothing! Another at the clock. Fourteen minutes past. Maybe the clock was wrong – fast? Now that was absurd. Mrs. Hilton managed a fleeting smile. The clock had been Frank's retirement present. Many years ago now. Reliable, dependable – solid was the word. Just like Frank had been. As she mused, watching the sunlight glowing on the rich mahogany of the clock case, she felt the unusual pang of guilt. The simple truth – there wasn't a great deal she remembered about Frank. Her memory of him had, sort of, faded over the years and now, sometimes, not always of course, she had trouble remembering his face. His cap, his pipe, the suit he only wore to funerals still in its plastic cover at the back of the wardrobe – but – his face? She sometimes had the curious detached feeling that he'd never really been there.

The clock chimed. Half past! A quick half desperate turn to the window now, on this frosty morning, clouded with condensation. She scoured it clean with the sleeve of her cardigan. The sudden movement provoked a sharp spasm of pain from the arthritic neck joint. Sleep tonight would be difficult. Glancing urgently through the cleared window she knew – beyond question she knew – that she hadn't missed him. Know – without knowing? This wasn't rational and she didn't like it. Mrs. Hilton was quite aware that some older people, and she wouldn't deny that she was an older person, that some of them do conjure up – fancies, foibles – become rather unbalanced emotionally. Often about men – sometimes men they barely knew. A thought that would have been disconcerting, except that Alice Hilton knew beyond all possibility of self-deception – knew empathetically – that she was not one given to romantic fantasising. She wasn't perfect – who was? No doubt she had her 'foibles' – possible some that other people were more aware of than she herself. But the core of her self-belief – forged and matured over a lifetime, was quite simple – she was a sensible and practical woman. Not a victim of – hot flushes – hormonal imbalances – mental incompetence – whatever! So, it galled her to be struggling with this overpowering feeling this fixation, if that was the word – for somebody she had seen only six – no seven – times through her parlour window standing across a short stretch of grass. Endlessly, and fruitlessly, she had churned over this absurdity – seeking to pin down some commonsense explanation – one that passed muster. What on earth reason could there be? Loneliness? Naturally, a logical reoccurring thought but, for her, laughably impossible. Daisy Ellis now – one of the regulars at the coffee group – she was lonely – at least that's what she told everybody. Daisy and Arthur had never got on – they hardly spoke – at least not to each other. But, from the day he died she rarely talked of anything else. She inserted, quite cheerfully, that she was 'lonely' – and there was no reason why she shouldn't enjoy it. Lonely? In search of companionship? The notion applied to her, Alice Hilton, really was ridiculous. There was the church, the coffee mornings – twice a week, children's society, French evening class, there was…! Whenever had she the spare time to even think about being lonely?

As for the thought that she filled her time curtain twitching – a busybody grabbing for titbits of gossip to pass on gleefully. Even more ludicrous. She was not a seasoned Harriet! Certainly, a good friend but it had to be said – a genuine busybody. Never malicious, of course, but a confirmed gossip. Long before what her nephew called social media all village tittle-tattle was channeled through Harriet – sometimes before it happened. But, certainly, no malice.

So, the situation and the speculation swirled around her mind – eddying back and forth – but all coming back to some mental cul-de-sac. Alice Hilton was possessed by a compulsive conviction with no key – no explanation.

She thought again of that first moment, incredibly, less than a week ago. It was 10 o'clock and she was cleaning the parlour window. The clock, Franks clock, had just chimed the hour. The last stroke died away as he, the stranger, and, yet, even in that first moment not quite a stranger, passed out of sight near the general stores. This she remembered vividly but, the next thing she recalled, with a shock of disbelief, was the clock striking again. Eleven! Eleven o'clock! She was still standing at the window cleaning cloth in hand. She had 'lost' an hour! Alice Hilton who never had enough minutes in the day had 'lost' an hour, and without the slightest remaining trace of any thought. Watching the telly in the evening she sometimes dropped off now and then, if it was a film or whatever she, literally, 'lost the plot'. That was evening times in the comfortable chair by a fire and not, unlikely a dram of 'something'. But in broad daylight, morning, standing cloth in hand cleaning a window! She recalled glaring accusingly at the clock as though somehow it, or possibly Frank, was playing a trick. What did remain was the powerful sense, that had stayed with her undiminished the entire week – the startingly clear awareness that this stranger was – somehow – important to her and that, somehow, she would be important to him. This conundrum had haunted every waking moment since and much of her troubled rest. No matter how she strove – wrestled – grappled – to resolve it – no success. Clairvoyance – telepathy – second sight – some quirk of the ether. These were nonsense. Alice Hilton was not, never had been, and had always resolved, never would be – superstitious. Some people certainly were. Leticia Greenwood for one. Another coffee morning devotee. Another stray thought – the 'coffee morning few' – now, possibly, including her, were an odd bunch, Leticia was intelligent, yet, tea-leaves, omens, 'intuitions' - she brimmed over with them. To be sure, she endured the good-natured banter of her friends with a knowing shrug. Her parting shot, which Mrs. Hilton now pointedly recalled, was unusually that they too – the skeptical three – would, at some point, confront 'the truth'.

The clock chimed. Mrs. Hilton's recollections ended abruptly in a sudden startling clarity. The tension had not just eased, it had gone – the fog of uncertainty and confusion along with it. It took a moment to adjust to this new psychological reality. Then, an enormous sense of relief. The clarity was that now she quite appreciated the danger to Mr. Keating, the reason he had not appeared today, and, the crucial part she now had to play. Momentarily, the stray thought of her frequent struggle with a difficult crossword. A really obstinate clue resolved only after a night's sleep when she often awoke with the solution. Mrs. Hilton felt an elation, almost a joy that her 'solution' had come – but after six – no seven – days and nights of mental anguish. Leticia would understand she thought wryly.

Conscious of the danger to - the stranger – Mr. Keating and its urgency Mrs. Hilton was also aware that she – and she alone – could help. That thought was a source of great happiness.

Briskly, but quite controlled, Mrs. Hilton stood up and pushed the heavy chair from its position in front of the window to its usual place near the bookcase. There was clear purpose but no clumsy haste and no panic. Her self-control seemed entirely natural, unforced and appropriate. Assuredly, she knew that, by some force, which she now had no desire to comprehend, she Alice Hilton was in command of events. In the hall, she pulled on her thick winter coat, wooly hat, gloves and the scarf her nephew had given her at Christmas. Outside, the driving winter wind tore at her breath as she leant into it and made her way steadily towards the High Street. As she turned into Lamb Lane there was a slight shudder of alarm and regret. Had she wasted an unnecessary hour sitting on that chair instead of...? Her clam returned. She felt assured that her feeling – her certainty – well – founded.

The cottage door was slightly ajar. Mrs. Hilton, with no hesitation, pushed the door open and went into the hall. Mr. Keating was lying quite still at the foot of the stair's, legs splayed at an awkward angle. There was a momentary spasm of shock. Mrs. Hilton had 'known' the danger and that there would be a serious problem but not exactly what it would be. However, her completed confidence in her 'mission', as she saw it, instantly returned. She crossed to him and walking briskly and competently, the way she did most things, checked Mr. Keating's pulse. Unconscious but alive, as she had known he would be, with a strong pulse. She put a coat under Mr. Keating's head otherwise touched nothing else and made the emergency call for an ambulance. Mrs. Hilton sat back on a lower step of the stairs. She felt quite at ease as she stared at Mr. Keating's inert body – she felt she'd had a sneak peek at the end of the story. For a fleeting moment of consciousness Mr. Keating's eyes met Mrs. Hiltons. He smiled then lapsed again into unconsciousness.

He did have a nice smile as Mrs. Hilton was quite sure he would.

In the ambulance the paramedic checked Mr. Keating again and said to Mrs. Hilton,

"He's very lucky you happened to be passing."

"Yes, wasn't it" said Mrs. Hilton with a smile.

40

The Past Does Not Equal The Future

Today is June 15th. The day had arrived! Soft and gentle – the warm promise of another summer as appealing as ever. Helen smiled faintly. Would rain have been better? Slanting rain blinding the eyes; a low sky crowded with black clouds; damp mist blanketing past and future. Now Helen laughed aloud to herself. Being fanciful at this time of the morning – with a day's work ahead.

Helen watched herself in the dressing table mirror. The smile had faded. There was some sadness in the grey eyes. Not enough to betray her feelings – but there all the same. She was annoyed as she recalled the firm resolution of the past few weeks.

What was remarkable about reaching forty? It was to be just another birthday. No different from thirty-nine or, even twenty- nine! By forty-one any excitement would be long forgotten. It was rather pathetic to be terrified by the thought or choose to laugh it off as a joke. The secret was not to believe there was something special about it. One didn't become a different person overnight – outwardly or inwardly.

This morning things had started well. George's most endearing quality as a husband was his sensitivity. He had understood. The children weren't a problem. At fifteen Jane was too preoccupied to be concerned about counting years. Phillip was six. He was ruled by his normal passions – breakfast and escaping from the house as quickly as possible.

Now they were all gone and Helen was sitting at the dressing table discontented. In spite of all her preparation the feeling was gaining hold that today was different. Helen reviewed her own strengths and weaknesses. One of the strengths was commonsense. This didn't mean she lacked strong feelings or wasn't totally feminine. But she also had control; a confidence in her own capacity to be calmly practical in most situations. Yet here she was – train in twenty minutes – on the point of giving way on one thing she had been determined about. Helen shrugged aside her disappointment and leaned much closer to the mirror. There was nothing new. No feature of her sun-browned face that wasn't completely familiar. She had never been pretty in a soft schoolgirl way. More striking. High cheekbones, lean face. The type of look that lasted, they said. Helen tilted her head to one side. No sagging around the jaw. The sparkling girl in the wedding photograph – nearly twenty years ago! – could have been her sister. Perhaps the face in the mirror was more mature. Helen smiled slightly. Maturity! Wasn't that just a painless way of admitting one was getting older?

Helen was subdued during the few minutes' walk to the station. For almost a year – since Phillip had gone to school – she had been working. This morning's walk to the train had represented her new freedom.

Helen had rarely felt frustrated by the routine of family chores. But going back to work after sixteen years was exciting – a new phase of her life. This morning the freshness was missing.

The train seemed more crowded than usual. In the crush at the station Helen had missed the girl-friend she normally travelled with. Chatting would have been an effort. She was glad to have escaped it. A middle-aged man gave up his seat to a rather attractive young girl with a vacant face standing next to her. Leaning against the door Helen watched the other passengers. First, she noticed the girls and younger women. They weren't all attractive. Some looked downright stupid. Surely even the modern generation of men would find them dull and lifeless. George could never had been attracted to any of these! Why use the past tense? Helen smiled at the thought of her husband going after another woman. But was it really incredible? His hair was thinning and he had put on more weight than she had but he wasn't stodgy. Why shouldn't some other women see the same qualities in him that she did? And why shouldn't he find some other women attractive? At that moment Helen's eyes rested on a girl sitting in a corner seat looking out of the window. Beautiful features, fresh complexion with only a skillful trace of make-up; long brown hair. The girl looked in her early twenties. She was sitting quite still, forehead leant against the window. She might have been asleep except for the sense of eager life which sparkled in the bright blue eyes. With a little shudder Helen dragged her gaze away from the girl and turned to look out of the window.

For a time, the early morning flood of typing swamped Helen's attention. Then her mind began to drift back towards the earlier thought. Mr. Pearson's charm seemed rather forced and artificial today. He was still polite but the new girl – much younger – received most of his attention. Helen wondered why she hadn't noticed before. The girl was really very young and rather naïve. Probably she couldn't see through his obvious line. Again, Helen felt irritated with herself and forced her attention back to the typing.

The other typist in the room was Mrs. Cox – Mary. Helen realised with a start that she was staring at Mary quite openly. She glanced back at her work. Poor Mary! Her husband had deserted her and the little girl some years before. But why 'poor Mary'? Helen forced herself to face the truth that Mary was as genuinely happy as anyone she knew. Looking up, Helen saw the friendly face, gentle eyes and the little smile as she put another sweet in her mouth. Mary didn't talk much about her marriage – but when she did mention it, she spoke quite openly in a matter of fact way. There couldn't be anything to regret when an unhappy relationship came to an end. The very worst thing must be for people to stay together making each other and the children miserable. Helen felt an odd mixture of satisfaction and unease on reaching this conclusion. She felt there could be something worse. The weary fruitily of life for the wife and mother taken for granted. A household objects. Part of the routine background of domestic life. Not really different from a washing machine or any other useful article. Perhaps not even aware of the emptiness as it grew until it became a vacuum surrounding the whole of life. Was there anything worthwhile to look forward to – apart from getting older? Wouldn't any other woman have been just as acceptable in her place?

Mary and Jill looked up in surprise as Helen jumped from her seat and rushed from the room. Helen controlled her rising emotion as best she could until she reached the ladies room. She locked the door, slumped into a chair and began to cry. Tears were rare with her and now they flowed freely as if to make up for lost time. As last she felt calmer. Automatically she took her handkerchief from her pocket and stepped to the mirror. She was stunned by the sorry ruin of tear stains and running make-up that stared back at her. The shock of her appearance set Helen's mind racing back over what had happened. Slowly the strained and smeared face relaxed into a grin. As the sense of her own absurd anxieties grew, Helen's grin exploded into laughter.

Everyone was anxiously attentive as a restored Helen reappeared in the typing room – even Mr. Pearson she noted with a smile. "Sorry!" she began. "Celebrating birthdays doesn't agree with me." A white lie was excusable. After a pause she added "especially when you reach the ripe old age of forty!" Quite happily she joined in the laughter…

The Double Life

Emily Marsden's legs ached. She was Seventy One years old and had been standing for twenty minutes in the middle of the concourse at Victoria station. A nervous unsteady obstacle directly in the path of a surging torrent of humanity. Mostly younger than she was – brimming with energy and purpose – the urgent need to be 'somewhere', to do, 'something', and do it yesterday. Emily also had a purpose, one that involved standing on this exact spot – directly under the large clock. She wasn't exactly clear why – except she knew she had to be there. 4.10! She was very early! One mustn't be late – not after fifty years.

The previous day had been remarkable – even for Emily whose double life was very, very remarkable. One that bought her continuing happiness and contentment, real fulfillment! Not the conventional double life at all! Not the sort her and Alice could sniff out – with her relentless hair trigger instinct for scandal. No furtive nerve – shredding half-life lived in the shadows – always on the knife-edge of discovery/ An accidental sighting here – an overheard telephone conversation there. Not a 'half-an-eye-over-the-shoulder' back alley double life. Emily had never needed to feel alarm that her friends might stumble upon her secret. One can't stub one's toe on something, literally, impossible – something so inexplicable and wonderful that there were moments she could hardly believe it herself. What Emily's friends did anguish about, from time to time, was why she had not married. Their occasional clumsy efforts at matchmaking were well-meaning – sometimes amusing, more often embarrassing – and all as sensible as driving full-speed down a cul- de-sac. They could not understand – how could they? Why their best efforts were rebuffed with amused – or irritated – tolerance.

"I'm perfectly, perfectly, happy!"

It didn't help that she obviously meant it.

At that point a man brandishing umbrella and briefcase like weapons barged into her. It may have been deliberate or because he was also reading a newspaper. At any rate he clearly felt the apology should come from Emily and glared venomously when it didn't. Emily sighed! 4.20! Still twenty-five minutes! The pain in her leg intensified but lessened as she thought of the startling events of yesterday.

Emily was one of that rare breed – unnatural to most people – who wake up ready to leap out of bed primed for the day ahead. Hit the ground running as they say. Yesterday was different. The instant she awoke she knew something had changed. She glanced around the room as if half-expecting an intruder – some visible change – furniture moved – articles rearranged on the dressing table. Everything was as usual – down to the empty cocoa mug on the bedside table. It was a beautiful autumn morning. Shafts of sunlight filtering through the slightly open curtains stirred by a gentle breeze from the window. A tranquil morning. The sort that carries the comforting assurance that everything is as normal. Yesterday morning was not like that. Emily was not superstitious – she was not given to premonitions – she didn't avoid ladders – she had never gazed hopefully into the depths of a crystal ball, but she was suddenly aware that something was different. A feeling – part excitement – part unease, that her life was, in some way, going to change. After fifty years on the same smooth highway of contentment – a turning point was coming. The unease was having no idea what the new direction might be. There was one certainty – something she knew had to be done – and urgently. Something, that only the day before she would have condemned as highly unprofessional. That same morning, she had resigned her job as personnel manager – no prior notice and no explanation. At least not one that would make any sense to an employer. She was excellent at her job – a thorough professional. She had the ideal qualities for a career in human relations–efficient with insight and compassion. Her firm had asked her – pleaded would be more accurate – to stay on beyond retirement. Emily happily agreed. Yesterday morning she announced bluntly she was leaving. Straight away! Permanently! And she did! On the pavement outside the office Emily had the compelling sense that she was engaged in a process of cutting the ties with her life to the present. Why – she had no idea!

Emily felt slightly dizzy. A slender solitary figure – a fragile island of stillness in the universal chaos around. An incessant battering of the senses, the overpowering incessant din) – trains – people – shouts – public announcements. 4.25! Only 4.25! Emily seriously doubted if she would survive the next fifteen minutes. Mercifully, she felt the uproar subside as she recalled the other incident of that remarkable day. Only yesterday! Five minutes in the morning to abandon a thirty-year career. Then the afternoon. She was in the spare bedroom – really a lumber room where anything and everything that didn't fall into the 'get rid of' category ended up. Emily liked a tidy house – she was fastidious - rather than finicky. The exception was the spare bedroom, not on the regular cleaning schedule. She couldn't remember why she went into that room or why – inexplicably – she chose to empty the top drawer of the old chest. Or how what she saw there – came to be there.

The lining of the drawer was a yellowing brittle-looking sheet of old newspaper – it's headlines in hold black type: "Miracle at Balham. One 1 dead…!"

Incredulity merged into shock. A headline reference to something banished from memory a lifetime ago. Then a surge of fierce indignation at seeing the death of her fiancé described as a miracle. She re-read the first paragraph.

"At 4.15pm yesterday, the 4.45 Dorking – Victoria train derailed at speed in Balham station. Despite extensive damage to train and station miraculously there is only one known dead – believed to be a man!"

The name of the man hadn't emerged until two days later.

Emily had known it the instant she heard the news over the tannoy at Victoria station. As she waited for a train that would never arrive and a man she would never marry.

"Believed to be a man!"

Emily recalled grief swamped by anger, 'believed to be a man?' a man? Any man? No, her man! Clive Forbes! Soft-spoken! Blue eyes! Infectious smile – always tinged with good humour. Emily realised she had never seen him out of khaki. She had joked the uniform seemed made for a man two sizes lager. He had joked that on army food he expected to grow into it. Clive! The man she had known such a cruelly short time. Three leaves! eleven days! Enough time to fall in love – laugh a lot – cry a little – quarrel once – war rationed happiness as well as cheese or fish! They became engaged on that last leave and decided marriage would come after the war.

"So, I'll have to come back, wont I?" she recalled his laugh.

And he did! On the 4.45 train, Dorking to Victoria. September 27th 1945. Fifty years ago.

There is a moment when shock gives way to profound emotional trauma. It was probably in that exact time when Emily had the germ of her idea. The idea that later blossomed in such an incredible way – into her double life. But first the unavoidable and impenetrable fog of desolation – diagnosed as a breakdown – and the referral to a psychiatrist. A very empathic man with a sad face - who seemed to have absorbed all the misery of his professional life. As much a victim of war as his patients. He was a good listener, to those willing and able to talk – but could offer little more than drugs and compassion. Emily accepted the compassion, she felt at times that he was the patient and she was there to ease his pain. The advice he gave was predictable and she made an effort to appear appreciative. 'She'll get over it!', 'she must look to the future', 'she was young and would meet someone else'. Emily had borne this glaring absurdity with a forced smile of thanks. That a piece of metal – a broken rail or whatever – could destroy their future? Absurd! And she had the powerful absorbing sense that their life would never – never become a mere memory – lodged with all the other debris – taken out and dusted – occasionally – increasingly faded and out of focus. Never destined to be a frozen image on a four inches by three inch piece of plastic. piece of plastic. Mooned over from time to time and less and less – until eventually, misplaced and forgotten. Never! Emily's mind utterly 'rejected' the mere thought that such a feeble charade could ever be acceptable. There would never be a ludicrous retreat into a comfort zone of escapist fantasy.

That was Emily's state of mine – of feeling – of passion. What happened next neither she nor Clive could ever, possibly account for. They lived a normal life – they grew old together over that vast stretch of time – watched television – disagreed over programmes, put out empty milk bottles. She darned stockings. Clive had a real gift for DIY. A double life – simple – natural. Emily could enter it – night or day – like opening a mental door – she left one reality – entered the other – and closed the door behind her.

Naturally, from time to time, they discussed possible explanations. The exercise had curiosity value, but that was all. It didn't really matter. Emily and Clive had no idea – and no way of knowing if their experience was unique. Emily sincerely, hoped that others like them, lives and hopes cruelly mangled by war would share their happiness. They didn't see themselves as special, in some way superior, more deserving. Neither were religious – not in any orthodox sense. Emily chose to see their life as a gift! From whom? Well, there were no name of sender – and no returned address. Clive called it a miracle! If that explained it – Emily wouldn't disagree.

"The train now approaching platform 5 is the 4.45 from Dorking!"

The distorted half unintelligible metallic crackle brought Emily back to the present and the need to be under that clock at 4.45! She was still uncertain why she was here. twenty seventh of September 1945. Emily simply did not have the mind set to remember – or commemorate – death – year after year. Especially where the victim was a man she had lived with – very happily- for fifty years. Still if the sensed, but vague, turning point in life required her to be here – here she had to be.

The urgency was very real but so now was the sudden wave of extreme fatigue and intensity of the ache in her legs. She had to have support. To the left was a newspaper kiosk. Emily half stumbled towards it and leant gratefully against the wall. She closed her eyes but jerked awake when a woman brushed against her. Long skirt…? Old fashioned thought Emily! And the hairstyle – pure Vera Lynn! If one waited long enough, time recycles things back into fashion. As Emily turned to return to her station under the clock, she caught sight of a young woman staring at her. Staring through a curious small window over a machine vending chocolate. Rather attractive – lipstick too emphatic – maybe a little vulgar – but it did suit her. Good eyes! The stare was bold – very direct and unflinching – rather puzzled curiosity than rudeness. The face seemed familiar. Maybe seen in a magazine. She was attractive enough.

"The train now arrived at platform 5 is the 4.45 from Dorking!"

She's be late! Emily felt she must move, but was held by the fascinating enigma of the familiar face. With an effort she broke the spell and turned. The same horde of restless humanity – but – uniformed. Uniforms – everywhere. Soldiers – in khaki mostly – some with shoulder feathers she couldn't recognise – a group of airmen and what nationality were those – looked like seamen. Some Americans – they always seemed better fed – chewing gum, of course. Civilians - collar and ties almost to a man. Women in the same retro fashion as the earlier one. Not a t-shirt, not a pair of jeans in sight! Not even a polo neck! A vast dizzying collage of movement and din suggesting some sprawling disorganised period fashion show – perhaps for charity or another thought – perhaps the crown on a film set.

Emily retreated to the wall for support. The young woman with the unflinching stare was still at the window. Now Emily began to smile. Of course, not a window, a mirror! The intense – now smiling woman with the vulgar lipstick was – Emily Marsden. At twenty-one! A face all but forgotten! Emily winked at her new friend in the mirror – now she understood the meaning of the turning point! She glanced at the big click and the place just below. A man – a soldier – had just spotted her. Had taken off his cap and waved it over the heads of the crowd. Emily had always liked the fire red colour of Clive's hair.

The End

Later On....Epilogue

The Narrator stopped just outside Trawden at a well-known vantage point to take a long look at the view of the village from the hill before he set off for the bus, he knew that this trip would be occurring far more regularly now. His visit had been a success and he felt physically and mentally agile once again and as if a stagnation in his life had suddenly been lifted, just like the preceding storm had now also gone.

He knew now that these people, Grandma, Great Uncle John, Great Auntie Emily, Auntie Edith, Uncle Arthur, they had passed in mortal terms but they were very much alive in the village and been there to help him. He smiled as he heard the voice "Lovely to see you back and don't leave it so long next time!" Whatever he had been through, life's difficulties, desperate times, lonely times, he had beaten them and triumphed over them and he was not lonely again.

It was time now for the Narrator to reveal his identity to the reader, he is Dan Reynolds and he has returned to Trawden and now is the time to undertake his biggest challenge, it's time to return to Telford...

R
LE

Dan Reynolds Returns To Telford

Dan Reynolds had not set foot in Telford for nearly forty years. This belated return visit wasn't planned or in any way premeditated though, later, he did come to feel there must have been some sort of subconscious impulse. Forty years before, at the age of twenty-two he had left the village for good. It was after University his mother had died six months before and there was no close family. There was no work to speak of in the village. To have any kind of future one had to leave – simple as that. Village life had come to seem oppressively claustrophobic – intrusive – no privacy. The pervasive unsettling feeling that everyone knew everything there was to be known about you – good and bad or made up! So, when the long-awaited moment came when one had to decide – the decision wasn't difficult.

The simple answer why he was heading that way was that he had been on an annual visit to Freda's sister Emily, who, unexpectedly, had to attend a friend's funeral.

Freda stayed at home with a bad cold but had insisted that he should go as usual. So, a full carefree spring day entirely at his disposal. He decided on a drive across the moors then a good put lunch – indulging his early retirement to the full. Feeling comfortably at ease with the world, and less comfortably at ease around the waist, he left the pub and headed back. After some miles he saw he had taken the wrong road. Later, he realized that the road he should have taken was plainly marked – in fact, impossible to miss. And yet – he had missed it. He stopped at the first signpost he met – Telford ten miles! It was oddly disturbing that the village was so, unexpectedly, near. When was the last time he had even thought of Telford? He sat staring at the sign post. The thought struck him that for over half his lifetime – the whole of his adult life in fact – he had fought shy of returning to Telford. Now a rag bad of dusty memories, heavily encrusted with age, scurried back to awareness. Dan brushed aside any hint of nostalgia – a weakness he'd always thought – a psychological 'fix' from the past to make the present more bearable. The point of living was to look forwards not backwards. There was a moment of wavering when he might have gone back. He didn't! He put the car into gear and headed towards the village.

Telford is a large village nestled in the foothills of the Pennines. No through road – essentially an industrial cul-de-sac created by the Industrial revolution. The mills were now closed, the tide of industry had receded leaving the village beached high dry without work. A dormitory village for people who worked elsewhere. Its location gave it the sense of a place isolated – cut off from the rest of the world. Maybe this sense gave the young Dan Reynolds one of his urgent reasons for leaving.

It's an exhilarating, even dramatic, drive across the moors on a fine day. This was lost on Dan who felt – unsettled. As though about to meet someone he had met years before and has no wish to meet again. He parked the car near the green which was, more or less, the centre of the village. Near the bus stop where the buses from the neighbouring town terminated. The place he had, as a boy and young man, come to regards, symbolically, as his route out – to the outside world, the future and a new life. It was here he used to catch the bus on his way to the grammar school at Fetcham. Sitting behind the wheel he could see that under aged twelve-year-old, satchel, with overlong straps, dangling about his knees. And in that satchel his mum's gastronomic masterpiece – her home-made chutney sandwich – the high point of his morning break. This he shared with Jimmy Captain whose mother lacked similar talent. Probably, it was the reason he always gave Jimmy the lion's share. Dan felt a sudden urge to know where Jimmy was, how was he, did he have a family, did he still live in Telford, could he come walking down that road ahead any minute – would he recognise him? Dan shook his shoulders feeling he needed to check this slide towards the quick sands of nostalgia.

He got briskly out of the car and started along the road towards the church in the distance. The road he had walked hundreds – thousands – of times. It struck him how little had changed. He felt a distant pleasure that Telford had, apparently, escaped the curse of piecemeal 'modernisation' – 'quantification' – or any other - 'action' -that sought to wrench a place from its moorings in history, strip it of character and identity and leave it just another name on a map. Not just pleasure an odd sense of pride that Telford had resisted all that! His gaze wandered to the weathered stonework of the cottages, the slate roofs, the rugged folds of the hills beyond with glimpses of heather, rising to an impressive skyline. His earlier self-young man or boy – must have stood at that very spot looking at the same scene and not 'seeing' it at all. Preoccupied, instead, with getting away. Understandable and for good reasons – yet missing the natural beauty of the place. It was as if he was seeing it for the first time. He felt he was flirting with nostalgia – again. Attentively he looked at the cottages. There was Maggie Thomson's. It looked bigger. Wasn't usual for things that seemed large in childhood to shrink in size as one gets older? Maggie!

A bustling old lady who did highly skilled needlework for her clients. 'Clients!' a modern clinical commercial word – an 'outsiders' word – cold, impersonal. Maggie did do paid work, but for neighbours, friends, family – the long-time residents of Telford – not a 'client' among them. His mother had a treasured table-cloth embroidered by Maggie. It would be nice to see it again! It nestled – protected, unused – in the bottom drawer of the cabinet in the front bedroom. To be brought out only on extra special occasions and, even then, shielded by a protective layer of paper mats. Dan now wished he had taken greater care at the house-clearing after his mother died. At the time he was clearing bric-a-brac – clutter – he saw now he was throwing out part of his own life history. He suddenly realised what it was about the size of Maggie's house. It had been enlarged – merged with the cottage next door. What had happened to the Drivers – who used to live there. Alf and Betty. Unaccountably, he felt add ended by the thought that he didn't know.

"Afternoon!"

A voice roused him from his reverie.

"Oh…afternoon!"

He replied reflectively, only really observing the man after he had gone by. A stranger! Well – after forty years almost inevitable! And yet…? Looking after the xxx figure – there was – something – about the set of the shoulders – and the walk? No – after a few moments he gave up – the memory – if it was genuine – refused to focus.

He continued his slow progress towards the church. Of course, there were changes – nothing, even a backwater, ever stands still. Colour for one thing! On both side of the road was a kaleidoscope of colour – window frames, doors, fences, garden gates. Yet there was no jarring clash – the whole pot pourri moulded into a natural harmony. His recollection of the road was – not exactly black and white – but – drab! Obviously, not everything could have been painted dark brown. Perhaps this memory too was darkened by his own unsettled mood at that period of his life. He spotted another change. A gap in the line of cottages. For some reason one had been taken down. That would have been, number twenty-four. Eddie Schofield! A small man – lived alone – always self-contained – private – as though jealously guarding a secret he thought might be snatched from him.

"How do!"

Another greeting caught him unaware – deep in thought about how startlingly vivid his memories were – seeming more sharply etched then even his neighbours back home. This greeting was from a much older man – and this time it wasn't overactive imagination – there was a momentary flash of recognition in the man's eyes. Dan was sure he knew the man – strip away the prosthetics of forty years.

"Hello!" He replied. The moment passed and the older man continued on his way. At the same moment someone came out of, number sixteen it was, on the other side of the road, no questions this time! Annie Foulds! Ten years older than he was – and the first great love of his life. He recalled the agony of that private passion –

impossible to declare of course – but endured in unrelieved and crushed isolation – and with the consistent fear of ridicule of defected by what he saw then and community thriving on gossip. He smiled, ironically at this thought – a village eager – even determined – to focus a cruel spotlight on the private emotional life of a fourteen-year-old schoolboy. He recalled his hopeful reassuring equation. That a ten year difference of age – fourteen to twenty-four shrank to insignificance at ages twenty to thirty! Then she married, thus creating the carefully constructed castles in the air. To a much older man – at least thirty years old. Dan closed the garden gate. It was all there! The cheerful round face, laughing eyes, that irresistibly dimples with age everything, miraculously still there. Her figure – well that had changed – she was – a word he only ever used with gentlemanly intent – matronly! She smiled at him as she spoke.

"Good afternoon!"

"Hello".

He scrutinised her face with an intensity he was afraid she mid find embarrassing, for any glimmer of recognition, none of course. Why should there be? There was the fleeting notion that at ages – sixty-two and seventy-two – the balance of advantage had switched in her favour. She noticed the smile – but not the cause – smiled back and moved off up the road to the bus terminal.

A car horn roused him from his latest reverie. The car had seen better days and was caked with mud. Probably a farmer from one of the outlying hill-farms- the ones who still drove horse and cart through the village when he was very young. The fresh-face of the robust young driver could only be the product of an out-door life. The man called out cheerfully:

"Sorry…thanks…morning!" and drove on.

Dan watched the car disappear with mild incredulity. Four times in less than ten minutes – three if you didn't count Annie as a stranger – strangers had greeted him – and in a friendly manner. What a contrast with Waring! He and Freda had move there two years before with the the repeated pleas of their daughter Ellen. In Waring it was possible – in fact normal – to walk from their house to the paper shop on to the general store come back via the green without a single soul offering a word of greeting. They were near Ellen, of course, but had never really settled. The house was fine though, certainly, too large for the two of them. It occurred to Dan that a cottage about the size of one of these would be ideal. Warring had all the amenities – as the estate agents say – shops, goo bus services, schools, pubs, church, coffee shops – including one that made the most delicious eclairs. A suburb – modern, clean, well-designed! Yet the parts – necessary important parts – didn't get into a coherent whole. Something was missing – and you were more aware of what was missing than what was there. Dan wasn't religious, like Freda but he thought, often, that maybe the word 'soul' disturbed what was missing. He had the sudden notion – the certainty – that, knock on any of these doors, the first words of the disturbed resident – dragged away from washing up, ironing, painting, whatever – would be – 'morning' or 'afternoon', 'hello' – not 'what do you want?' Spoken with suspicion and some menace. As he stood milling over his thought, he glimpsed another familiar sight – over the roofs of the cottages. The old Methodist chapel, with its obligatory, his mother insisted, Sunday morning bible classes. Time spent acquiring a ragbag of biblical prints- of which fragments remained – the old testament prophets, the sequence of old and new testament books, the twenty third psalm – the rather impressive verses about sounding brass and tinkling cymbals

Memory, Dan reflected, can be overwhelming if you give it free rein – but knowing that is much easier than slamming on the brakes, he was finding it increasingly difficult to reconcile the Telford of memory and the Telford of the here and now. It was a risk he'd been hazily aware of from the moment he swung the car into the Telford road – a road in to the past but maybe, also the future. Dan felt that for forty years he'd harboured a sort of threadbare memory cobbled together from a heavily slanted version of village life. Slanted by the angst of a teenage boy and young man hell-bent on escape. Every nuance of village life seen through the retracting lens of their preoccupation. Dan understood the motive – but it was of its time and place and missed so much.

"Excuse me!"

It was the man who had first greeted him on arrival in the village. Dan's first impression that he knew the man hardened into a certainty.

"It is Dan, isn't it? Dan Reynolds?"

"Yes…er…"

"You don't remember me?"

"Certainly, I do, I'm sorry, the name…"

"Alan Flowers!"

Instantly, complete recognition flooded back – in the same class at primary school. Alan sat in the back corner near the window always getting caught by Miss Shaw for staring out – good at mental arithmetic – couldn't spell – great at football – always seemed to slam the ball straight between the goal posts marked out in white paint on the school wall…

"Alan, of course! How are you?"

"Fine, never moved far – from James street, remember, to Newton Terrace, all of half a mile. I haven't got much time Dan, that's my bus".

He pointed to a bus at the terminal

"But I wanted a quick word, I was thinking of you just this morning"

"Me?"

"you're not leaving straight away, are you?"

"Well, no, not straight away"

Alan stared at Dan with a puzzled grin then continued.

"It's weird – you coming here today. I mean today of all days! I mean, why did you come? Did you have any particular reason, any, feeling?"

"no, well, er, I couldn't call it a…"

"I mean the thing only went up yesterday. Course that made me think of you then bless me, this morning - scouts honour – I had the feeling you might be back. Look, I've got to go – the bus will wait for me but not for long. Anyway, you go up to the old place, you know where I mean?"

Dan nodded quite bemused, torn between trying to think of some suitable reply and laughing out loud.

"Must go! Don't forget, the old place! I'll see you later, I hope. What a coincidence though".

With that he hared off along the road with a speed that, as a fellow sixty-odd year old, Dan could only envy.

He knew every inch of the remaining stretch of road to the Church and the path around the Church yard that led to cross lane. He hastened along anxious for the explanation to Alan's cryptic comments. As he turned the familiar corner he stopped abruptly – and understood.

There was the cottage. Home for twenty-two years. Shrouded by a much more luxuriant growth of foliage than he remembered. Matured and stronger with age but a lot of trimming might help. And there was the sign!

"For Sale"

Dan knew instantly, no further reflection was needed – as though the sign had been the catalyst to crystallise as a maturing line of thought. He took out his mobile phone. Freda had to be contacted. But, first things first – he read the details from the sign.

"0…1…7…6…5…3…2…1…4"

As he awaited the response he thought, "Coincidence", Alan had said "maybe…maybe?"

The End

www.ingramcontent.com/pod-product-compliance
Lightning Source LLC
Chambersburg PA
CBHW041923180726

48295CB00002B/54